# The Weightlifter's Laughter

## and other funny poems by Colin West

Book Guild Publishing
Sussex, England

First published in Great Britain in 2011 by
The Book Guild Ltd
Pavilion View
19 New Road
Brighton, BN1 1UF

*The Wandering Bear* by Colin West
Text © 1996 Colin West
Reproduced by permission of Walker Books Ltd, London SE11 5HJ
www.walker.co.uk

*The King's Toothache* by Colin West
Text © 1987 Colin West
Reproduced by permission of Walker Books Ltd, London SE11 5HJ
www.walker.co.uk

*I Bought My Love A Tabby Cat* by Colin West
Text © 1988 Colin West
Reproduced by permission of Walker Books Ltd, London SE11 5HJ
www.walker.co.uk

Printed in Great Britain by
CPI Antony Rowe

A catalogue record for this book is available from
the British Library.

ISBN 978 1 84624 592 3

The Weightlifter's Laughter

Colin West obtained a diploma in graphic design and then studied illustration
at the Royal College of Art, when he also started to write humorous verse,
influenced by Roger McGough, Ogden Nash and Edward Lear. His first
collection of verse, *Out of the Blue from Nowhere*, was published a year after he
obtained an MA. He has illustrated books by Michael Rosen, Helen Cresswell
and Paul Stewart, and his own successful *Jungle Tales* from 1986 are still in
print. His book *Monty the Dog Who Wears Glasses* was made into a cartoon
series by the BBC, and his poems have appeared in over a hundred anthologies.
In 2009 his work was featured in the CBBC series *Poetry Pie*. He is married
and lives in a former laundry in Epping, where he boasts a huge collection of
mainly nonsense verse. His popular website is at www.colinwest.com.

9030 00001 8999 2

**Other books of verse by Colin West:**

Out of the Blue from Nowhere
Back to Front and Back Again
Not to be Taken Seriously
A Step in the Wrong Direction
It's Funny When You Look at It
A Moment in Rhyme
The Best of West
What Would You Do with a Wobble-Dee-Woo?
Between the Sun, the Moon and Me
Long Tales, Short Tales and Tall Tales
The Big Book of Nonsense
A Crocodile's Teeth

**As editor:**
The Land of Utter Nonsense
The Beginner's Book of Bad Behaviour
The Bestest Ever Bear

# Remember . . .

you can write a poem
on the back of an envelope,
in an old exercise book,
on a computer,
or in bed.
You can write a poem . . .
on a piece of parchment,
in a classroom,
on a whim,
in a hurry,
on a bus,
or in your head!

# Contents

# The Weightlifter's Laughter

After the weightlifter lifted one weight,
He waited, then lifted another . . .
With both weights aloft,
Then the weightlifter laughed—
From tickles inflicted (as here is depicted)
By someone who looks like his mother.

# The Baby's Lament

When Mum puts on
My nappy tight,
I somehow lose
My appetite!

# My Hairstyle

My hairstyle
is a rare style:
a crop
on top,
a quiff
sprayed stiff,
the left side
I've dyed
snowy white,
while the right
is the blackest of black,
and a ponytail
hangs at the back!

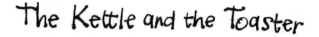

# The Kettle and the Toaster

A kettle loved a toaster,
But the toaster didn't care.
The kettle whistled loudly
To show that it was there.

The kettle blew its top off
And got extremely hot,
But the toaster wasn't turned on,
So het up it was not!

# An ABC of Tragedy

**A was an Archer**
who filled me with fear

**B was a Barber**
who cut off my ear

**C was a Chemist**
who poisoned my tea

**D was a Doctor**
who hammered my knee

**E, Electrician**
who gave me a shock

**F was a Fighter**
who knocked off my block

G was a Ghostie
or was it a Ghoul?

H, a Headmaster
who called me a fool

I was an Infant
who made me feel sick

J was a Jester
who gave me a kick

K was a King
who was bad as can be

L, Lumberjack
whose tree fell on me

M a Magician
who sawed me in two

N was a Nutcase
who lived in my loo

O was an Oarsman
in whose boat I sank

P was a Pirate
who said Walk the plank

Q was a Queen and
she chopped off my head

R was a Robber
who filled me with lead

S was a Stranger
who stole all he could

T was a Tailor
who stitched me up good

U, Unicyclist
who knocked me down flat

V was a Villain
who kidnapped my cat

W, a Werewolf
who had awful breath

And X, Y and Z,
they just bored me to death.

# Who's Ugliest?

A warthog and a wildebeest
Were wondering one day
Between them who was the ugliest,
When who should come their way,
But Mr Hippopotamus,
Which prompted them to say:
'Aha, it's neither one of us,
Three cheers, hip hip hooray!'

# Riding to School

I wouldn't half laugh if I saw a giraffe
Riding to school on a scooter,
And even more funny would be a big bunny
Following, honking his hooter.

# The Story of Walter Wilde

A prodigy was Walter Wilde
(Which means he was a gifted child):
Just ten weeks after he was born,
Up he got and mowed the lawn.

He gave the garden fence a coat
(At eighteen months) of creosote,
And by the time that he was three
He'd fixed the broken-down TV.

Remarked his mother to her spouse:
'Our lad seems handy round the house.
We maybe should advantage take—
Think of the money we could make!'
So thus they advertised their son:
COME GET YOUR HOUSEHOLD JOBS ALL DONE.

And soon they hired out little Walt,
Who proved hardworking to a fault.

He grouted
tiles and mixed
cement . . .

. . . and
mended bikes
whose wheels
were bent . . .

He painted . . .

. . . plumbed . . .

. . . and plastered too . . .

There seemed no task he couldn't do,
But come the day, as comes to all,
When Walter had to go to school . . .

The teachers there were rather riled
To see such exploited a child.
They longed to *educate* the kid
(For after all, that's what they did).

They longed to teach him how to spell
And how to read and write as well,
To teach him how to multiply,
And all about square roots and pi.
But all the same, Miss Meek (the Head)
Took Walter to one side and said:

'It seems the
old school
boiler's burst.
Walt, maybe
you could fix
it first?'

# Answerless Questions

Is it a Cucumber's dream
To one day be a Marrow?

Is it a Feather's fancy
To be fixed upon an Arrow?

*Do* Caterpillars fantasise
About becoming Butterflies?

Is it possible a Carrot
Could prefer to be a Parrot?

Do Octopuses wish
They might be Jellyfish?

(As though I haven't got enough
To think about, without this stuff!)

# Losing My Mind

As I was fishing at the well
I lost my mind and down it fell.
Deep down within that hole so black,
It plummeted, alas alack!
All I could do was stand and stare
To see it disappear down there,
And then to hear, with gentle thud,
It come to rest upon the mud.
Alone now, with my rod and line,
I'm fishing for that mind of mine.

# The Old Kitchen Sink

When we moved house,
We took everything—
My mother's old apron,
My auntie's fake mink,
Four cups and saucers,
And one odd cuff link,
And several bottles
Of Indian ink.

We took the old washstand
That was painted bright pink,
Our old garden hosepipe
(With many a kink),
And Granny's old bathtub
(The one made of zinc),
And two pairs of socks
Which had started to shrink.

We loaded the van
And were just on the brink
Of leaving, when Grandad
Remarked with a wink,
'That's the lot, now I'm sure
That we've got everyfink!'
Then chuckled, 'Except for
The Old Kitchen Sink!'

But Grandad's remark
Made me suddenly blink;
It stirred up my mind
And I started to think
That never again
Would I get me a drink
From the cold water tap
Of the old kitchen sink,

17

# Connie Cook

Pray spare a thought for Connie Cook
Whose nose was always in a book,
She'd still be here amongst us if
She hadn't walked so near a cliff.

# Philip Fox

Remember also Philip Fox
Whose hobby was collecting rocks;
If Connie hadn't squashed him flat,
He'd be here too and not gone *splat*!

# Advice

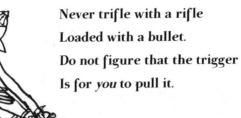

Never trifle with a rifle
Loaded with a bullet.
Do not figure that the trigger
Is for *you* to pull it.

Likewise shun a Gatling gun,
a dagger or machete,

And catapults are just for dolts
(Unless you meet a Yeti).

# The Wandering Bear

Once upon a time a bear
Wandered here and wandered there;
Upon his face he wore a frown,
For walking seemed to get him down.
One day he stopped and said, 'I know,
I'll buy myself some skates,' and so . . .
He saved up hard and soon he bought
Some lovely skates, or so he thought . . .

He used his skates and for a while
Upon his face he wore a smile,

But then he thought, 'I'd really like
To ride around upon a bike.'
And so he saved up hard and bought
A lovely bike, or so he thought . . .
He rode his bike and for a while
Upon his face he wore a smile.

But then he thought, 'I could go far
If I had my own motor car.'
And so he saved up hard and bought
A lovely car, or so he thought . . .

He drove his car and for a while
Upon his face he wore a smile.
But then he thought, 'I'd rather float
Upon the water in a boat.'
And so he saved up hard and bought
A lovely boat, or so he thought . . .

He sailed his boat and for a while
Upon his face he wore a smile.
But then he thought, 'I'd rather fly
An aeroplane high in the sky.'
And so he saved up hard and bought
A lovely plane, or so he thought . . .

He flew his plane and for a while
Upon his face he wore a smile.
But then to his surprise he found
He missed his life back on the ground.
And so he sold his aeroplane
And then went shopping once again.
He bought some hats and socks and suits,
And last of all, a pair of boots.

And now he is a happy bear
Who wanders here and wanders there.
And as he goes from place to place,
A smile is always on his face.

# What Colour?

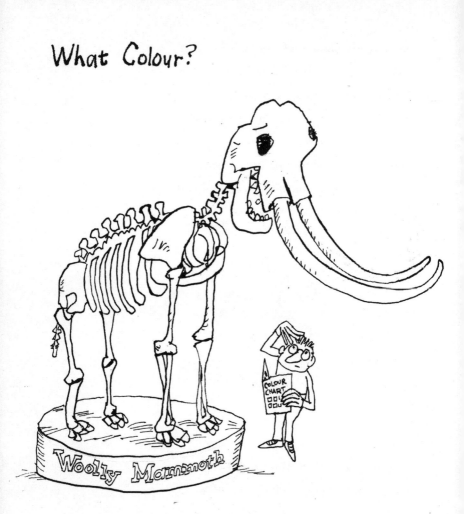

O, its bones may be colossal
But the trouble with a fossil
Is that it doesn't give a clue
As to the creature's actual hue.

Take that Diplodocus fellow
Was he green or blue or yellow?
And was Tyrannosaurus Rex
Perhaps adorned with spots or checks?
And it may seem quite irrelevant,
But that prehistoric elephant,
The Woolly Mammoth, what d'you think,
Purple, puce or shocking pink?

# A Brighton Ballad

'Tell us, tell us, Grandad,
How off you went to war
And fought the Battle of Brighton
In 1964 . . .'

Well, we rode down on our scooters
On that Bank Holiday,
We tooted on our hooters
And folk got out the way!

Our headlights were a-gleaming,
Our mirrors, they were too;
On each and every aerial
A Union Jack we flew.

26

Now, when we got to Brighton
And went along the Prom,
There came a horde of Rockers,
Lord only knows where from!

I'll tell you of them Rockers—
They drove us up the pole—
'Cos we liked Motown music,
While they liked rock 'n' roll.

And up against that rabble,
They weren't a pretty sight,
With bottles at the ready
And looking for a fight . . .

27

It started just with jeering
(It might have been the booze),
Then someone yelled a war cry
And soon all hell broke loose.

We set about them Rockers
(We didn't know no fear!)
We pelted them with pebbles
And chased them up the pier.

But as I grabbed one greaser,
His girlfriend took offence:
She hit me on the helmet
And left a lot of dents.

I fell, but that fair lady,
She held me in her arms,
She cradled me and told me
She hadn't meant no harm.

'Twas then I had a vision,
And saw that it was wrong
To pick a fight with someone
When folk should rub along.

We slipped away together
(She gave her boy the boot),
With her dressed in her
leathers
And me in my mod suit.

And being with that woman,
My new life soon began:
The next year we got married—
That girl is now your nan.

'Thank you, thank you, Grandad,
For telling us once more
Of how you met our granny
In 1964!'

# Bubblegum

Bubblegum is troublesome
When stuck upon your sole.
Tread carefully and prayerfully
If going for a stroll.

# My Favourite Things

(With apologies to Oscar Hammerstein II)

Teachers with measles
With spots on their noses,
Ferrets and weasels
And prickles on roses,
Vile vampire bats
With umbrella-like wings,
These are a few of *my* favourite things.

Spindly grasshoppers
And custard with lumps in,
Great big gobstoppers
And puddles I jumps in,
Watching the way
That a jellyfish stings,
These are a few of *my* favourite things.

(When the sun shines,
When the bird sings,
When I'm feeling mad,
I simply remember
My favourite things,
And then I don't feel so bad.)

Clothes that are sloppy
And *not* doing homework,
Dad's old jalopy
With rust on its chromework,
Burning reports
That the end of term brings,
Yes, these are a few of *my* favourite things!

# My Cat

My cat's so much a mass of fur,
I'm not sure if it's him or her.

# Humphrey Hudson

Humphrey Hudson MA (Oxon)
Goes to bed with just his socks on
I think it must be rather chilly
Wearing nothing on your ... tummy.

# The Backpacker's Picnic

A backpacker packing a picnic
Picked up his backpack to pack.

He popped in a pippin,
A pork pie, some pickle,
A packet of peanuts
And pineapple pop.

With picnic now packed up,
The backpacker picked up
His backpack to put on his back.

# Some New Nursery Rhymes

## I

Hey diddle diddle,
The cat smashed his fiddle,

The cow pulled a face
at the moon,

The little dog snored
Because he was bored,

And the dish had a fight
with the spoon.

# 2

I had a pet piranha fish, nothing would it eat
But a fair princess's hand and her dainty feet.
The King of Spain's daughter I served up on a dish,
And all for the sake of my pet piranha fish.

# 3

Little Miss Muffet sat on a tuffet,
Eating a fabulous lunch
It wasn't a spider who sat down beside her,
But seventeen bears in a bunch.

# Crossword

Can you make sense of this crossword poem?
The solution is shown upside down!

Crosswords are really
great fun filling in,
Just make up the answers
and always you'll win.

# Dodgems

I
put
my
foot
down
really
HARD

when I drive a dodgem car

and off I go

(I'm never slow)

I
feel
like
I'm a
star!

I twist and spin the car I'm in

round corners really tight

and
other
cars

caught
in a
jam

I RAM
WITH ALL
MY MIGHT!

# Sophie's Punishment

'Oh, Sophie, dear, I do not think
Papa would care a lot
To see the way with pen and ink
You always leave a blot.

If you could only hold the pen
Between your fingers *so*,
You'd write less clumsily, and then
The ink would freely flow.'

Mamma then made some marks inside
The little copybook,
And viewed her work of art with pride,
And bade her child to look.

But Sophie, mischief in her eyes,
Believed it might be fun
To ridicule and criticise
The work Mamma had done.

And so the daughter, stern of face,
Observed her mother's script,
And screamed, 'This is a sad disgrace.
I ought to have you whipped.'

At such an insolent remark
Mamma was not amused
To take her daughter to the park
Next day she quite refused.

And though the sun was scorching hot,
Mamma would not relent.
To write all day without a blot
Was Sophie's punishment.

# I Bought My Love a Tabby Cat

I bought my love a tabby cat,
A tabby cat, a tabby cat,
My love made him a velvet hat
To wear when we were wed.

I bought my love a billy goat,
A billy goat, a billy goat,
My love made him a woolly coat
To wear when we were wed.

I bought my love a big fat pig,
A big fat pig, a big fat pig,
My love made him a fancy wig
To wear when we were wed.

I bought my love an old grey goose,
An old grey goose, an old grey goose,
My love made him some dainty shoes
To wear when we were wed.

I bought my love a little mule,
A little mule, a little mule,
My love made him a silken shawl
To wear when we were wed.

I bought my love a talking crow,
A talking crow, a talking crow,
My love made him a pretty bow
To wear when we were wed.

And on the day that we were wed,
That we were wed, that we were wed,
I turned to my true love and said,
'Oh, what a sight to see . . .

'A tabby cat
who wears a hat . . .

'. . . a billy goat
who wears a coat . . .

'. . . a big fat pig
who wears a wig . . .

'. . . an old grey goose
who wears new shoes . . .

'. . . a little mule
who wears a shawl . . .

'. . . and a talking crow
who wears a bow . . .

46

'Oh, heaven help us, who's to say,
Oh, who's to say, oh, who's to say,
Who is the finest dressed today
It's anyone but me.'

But since that day when we were wed,
When we were wed, when we were wed,
My love makes clothes for me instead,
As handsome as can be!

# Cats and Dogs

Would you rather have a moggy than a doggy?
Would you rather hear a purr than hear a yap?
Would you rather stroke a feline than a canine?
Would you rather have a cat upon your lap?

or

Would you rather have a 'Towser' than a mouser?
Would you rather go for walks than stay at home?
Would you rather hear a bowwow than a miaow?
Would you rather have a dog who likes to roam?

# Washing Up

I really hate it when I go
To do the washing up,
And turn the tap a *bit* too hard,
And in the bowl a cup
Is in the very very place
The gush of water goes,
Which splashes water EVERYWHERE,
But mostly up my nose.

# Greedy Nelly

On a picnic, greedy Nelly
Demonstrated eating jelly,
And we'd all have been so grateful
Had she only ate a plateful.

But she wasn't quite so thrifty,
And her helpings numbered fifty.
Such a large amount of jelly
Took its toll on greedy Nelly:
She came over queer and queasy
And found standing far from easy.

She began to quake and quiver
And fell in a nearby river;
On the banks we stood there thinking
That poor Nelly should be sinking,
But her stomach proved so bloated,
That she didn't sink, but floated.

So we hauled her from the river,
And as she began to shiver,
We prepared a celebration
Full of joy and jubilation.
All night long we danced round Nelly
Singing songs unto her belly.
O what mayhem we created
As she gradually deflated!

# Funny Bone

It's true I have a funny bone
(We all have, I believe),
It's just that I don't show it off,
I keep it up my sleeve.

# Stan the Goldfish

I have a goldfish, name of Stan,
Who has a short attention span:
So short, that when you call his name,
He comes, then wonders why he came.

# Love Poem

I do like me
an awful lot,
think of the
qualities I've got—
I'm humble, honest,
handsome too,
and more fun being with
than you.

I'm cool, considerate
and kind,
and when I think
of me, I find
the word 'perfection'
comes to mind.

I'm super, splendid,
stylish, sweet
I'm nimble, noble,
nice and neat.
I'm playful,
plucky and polite
I'm brainy,
brilliant and bright.

    (And yet, although
    my ways are such,
    no one seems to
    like me much.)

# The Tale of Robert Bligh

Behold the youthful Robert Bligh
Who liked to watch the trains go by.
He was a very thorough lad;
He'd jot their numbers in a pad,
Then neatly add the Time and Date
And 'tut' if one was running late.

Now, this young
fellow lately had
Been given by
his wealthy dad
A rather fancy
camera,
Which made him hoot
and howl 'Hurrah!'

He snapped away with great delight
At almost anything in sight,
And every photograph he took
He pasted in a pretty book,

One morning Robert thought that he
Might thus preserve for all to see
The famous 7.22
Express train out of Waterloo,
Which daily passed his favoured spot
At seven thirty on the dot.

And so it was
he did unpack
His camera
beside the track,
And set the shutter
speed to fast
To snap the train
as it went past . . .

As Robert waited for the train,
A notion popped in to his brain:
'How much improved the shot should be
If it could also feature *me*.
How lovely, when the loco came,
If I were also in the frame.

And furthermore, how proud of me
My generous papa would be!'

He set the button to *delay*
So he'd have time to make his way
Before the lens, and thus to be
Included in the snap, you see.
He waited then with bated breath
For that Waterloo express.

At last the train came into sight
O how the boy danced with delight!

Then knowing he
could clearly hear
The locomotive
*very* near,
He pressed the knob
and jumped out quick
In good time for
the shutter's click.

Rob proved *too* keen, alas, alack!
He'd rashly leapt on to the track.
How tragic! Yet (one shouldn't laugh)
It made a super photograph.

# Flat

In Norfolk alone in a cornfield
A ruminative fellow once sat
Surveying that rather forlorn field
And noticing how it was flat.

'When I were a nipper,' he pondered,
'We'd always a hillock or two,
And ranges wherever we wandered
With peaks like the ones in Peru.

'We'd cliffs and we'd crags and we'd mountains,
Of flatness there wasn't a trace
We'd spouting volcanoes and fountains
And ridges all over the place.'

The fellow then rose from his hummock,
But, all of a sudden, he slipped,
And soon he was flat on his stomach,
As over a molehill he'd tripped.

# The Sofa and the Rocking Chair

The sofa sighed to the rocking chair:
'I wish I could be more like you,
And tap in time to the beat of a rhyme
And send to sleep the person who
Sits in my arms as you do.'

The rocking chair said to the sofa:
'How I wish I could do what *you* do—
To not be so rootless and restless
And seat not one person, but two—
I'd happily give up my rocking
If I could be steadfast like you.'

# The Proud Parents

A very proud pair of parents
Was Brian and Briony Bruce
Who pushed their Polly in a pram
Round Ashby-de-la-Zouch.

But then one fateful Saturday
The vicar pointed out
That what they took for Polly was
In truth a Brussel sprout.

O shame upon that clergyman
To do the thing he did!
What harm was there to let them think
Their vegetable a kid?

# My Pterodactyl

Once I had a pterodactyl
And I kept him in a shack till
He escaped. Alas, alack! Till
He comes back, my world is black till
Then with pain I shall be racked, till
He comes back, my pterodactyl.

# The King's Toothache

At Kennelwick Castle,
Gadzooks and forsooth,
The king has a terrible
Ache in his tooth.

'Go fetch me a dentist,'
He moans to his nurse,
'And hurry up, Mary,
Before it gets worse.'

So Mary, she gallops
To nearby St Ives
To fetch him a dentist,
But when she arrives,

She looks left and right,
And she looks up and down,
But there's not one dentist
In all of the town.

So Mary, she stands
And she scratches her head,
And decides to return
With the baker instead.

At Kennelwick Castle
The king's tooth still aches.
The baker comes in
With a trayful of cakes.

The king eats them up,
But they don't do the trick;
His tummy now aches
And he's feeling quite sick.

'Go fetch me a doctor,'
He moans to his nurse,
'And hurry up, Mary,
Before it gets worse.'

So Mary, she gallops
To nearby St Ives
To fetch him a doctor,
But when she arrives,
She looks left and right,
And she looks up and down,
But there's not one doctor
In all of the town.

So Mary, she stands
And she scratches her head
And she decides to ask back
The town crier instead.

At Kennelwick Castle
To make the king well,
The town crier lets out
A deafening yell.

The king isn't cured, though,
And takes to his bed,
For now he's complaining
Of aches in his head.

'Go fetch me a surgeon,'
He moans to his nurse,
'And hurry up, Mary,
Before it gets worse.'

So Mary, she gallops
To nearby St Ives
To fetch him a surgeon,
But when she arrives,
She looks left and right,
And she looks up and down,
But there's not one surgeon
In all of the town.

So Mary, she stands
And she scratches her head,
And decides to go back
With a sailor instead.

At Kennelwick Castle
The sailor he looks
Deep down the king's mouth,
And with twine and with hooks,
He gets hold of the tooth,
Which he waggles about,
Then he tugs on the string
And he pulls it clean out.

He then pours a potion,
And though looking glum,
The king drinks it down
And it cures his bad tum.

Then singing a shanty
And dancing a jig,
The king throws his headache
Away with his wig.

He hasn't a worry,
He hasn't a care,
He's fit as a fiddle
And dancing on air.
'Three cheers for the sailor
For all that he's done
A dentist and doctor
And surgeon in one!'

# Some Clothes

Some clothes are in the cupboard
But there's one thing for sure
Raincoats, frocks and dresses
Aren't what I'm looking for.

Some clothes are in the cupboard,
And some are in a drawer
But knickers, vests and hankies
Aren't what I'm looking for.

Some clothes are in the cupboard,
And some are in a drawer,
And some are hanging on a hook
Upon my bedroom door
But a nightie and a dressing gown
Aren't what I'm looking for.

Some clothes are in the cupboard,
And some are in a drawer,
And some are hanging on a hook
Upon my bedroom door,
And some are lying on my bed,
And underneath are more
But slippers, shoes and sandals
Aren't what I'm looking for.

Some clothes are in the cupboard,
And some are in a drawer,
And some are hanging on a hook
Upon my bedroom door,
And some are lying on my bed,
And underneath are more,
And some are even piled in heaps
Which cover all the floor.

Yippee! My witch's outfit!
*That's* what I'm looking for!

# Scone

In Richmond (Yorks)
As the sun shone,
I went to the baker's
And bought me a scone.

I travelled down south,
And then all alone
In Richmond (Surrey)
I ate that scone.

# Dictionary

Now here's a book to help you write,
With all the words you'll need.
If you should read but just one book,
Make this the one you read.

You only have to take some words
At random from its pages,
And you could be an author too
Whose work lives through the ages.

Just think now, every single word
That Dickens wrote is herein,
So go pick up this hefty tome
And take some time to peer in.

Keats, Shakespeare, Chaucer, Tennyson,
Their words are too included,
So take a leaf from out of their books,
You'll be so glad that you did.

# Granny's Greens

My granny grows the biggest veg
That I have ever seen.
There's no one in the whole wide world
Whose fingers are so green.

She needs
*massive* pots
to grow her
shallots . . .

. . . and cans
with huge
spouts
to water her
sprouts . . .

. . . and
*humongous*
hoes
to tend her
bean rows . . .

. . . and *gigantic* barrows

to carry her marrows . . .

Yes, Granny grows the biggest veg

That I have ever known—

And the balcony of Granny's flat

Is where it all is grown!

# Two Books at Once

Charles Dalrymple, he's no dunce,
He likes to read two books at once—
He holds a book in either hand,
The words by separate eyes are scanned—
In his left is Enid Blyton,
In his right, he's got his sight on
A grisly book of Roald Dahl's,
O, what a clever boy is Charles!*

*For thinking so, you'd be excused,
But Charles, alas, he gets confused,
So don't ask him to tell to you
The tales he reads, for if you do,
It's likely that your ear he'll bend
With tales of Noddy's gruesome end.

# Round the Campfire

When I was a boy scout
Sitting round the campfire,
We made each other freak out
With stories of a vampire:
A vampire on the lookout
For boy scouts round a campfire
Who made each other freak out
With stories of a vampire . . .

# The Obstreperous

Beware the Obstreperous,
It comes out at night . . .

It's hideous and horrid and hairy!
Its horns are a horrible sight
It's scruffy and scabby and scary
It grows to a humongous height.

It's scratchy and scummy and scaly,
And boy, can its mandibles bite!
Its cry is all warbly and waily,
It's freaky and gives you a fright!

Beware the Obstreperous,
IT'S COMING TONIGHT!

# Wallabagoo

I'm glad that I live here in Wallabagoo,
There's always a zillion things you can do—
You can lie in the shade of a Tippety Tree
And watch as a Bottle Bee lands on your knee,
You can sip a Zonata or nibble a Nog
Or hear the far call of the wild Jitterjog.

It's better than living in Mumble-on-Murk,
For when you live there, all you do is hard work—
There are Fiskets to fill up and Coggles to turn,
And seventeen Scrudles a year's all you earn.
Yes, happy am I here in Wallabagoo.
I bet that you'd like to be living here too!

# Fact or Fiction?

William Tell took aim so well,
His arrow split the apple,
His little boy, he jumped for joy
And gave thanks in the chapel.

Dick Turpin wasn't
half as good
as poor man's hero
Robin Hood.
Like Hood, he stole
the rich man's wealth,
but kept the booty
for himself.

Robert the Bruce
Thought 'What's the use?'
Until he eyed a
Spider.

Observing how an apple fell,
Sir Isaac let out quite a yell
'If things fell up, not down,' he said,
'I wouldn't have so sore a head.'

# Two Limericks

A very fat turkey named Reggie
At Christmas became rather edgy:
He was huffin' and puffin'
At the mere thought of Stuffin'
How he wished everyone was a 'veggie'.

He ate up all the pies, did Sidney,
Then sadly, he EXPLODED, didn'e?
The pitch, no mistake,
Was spattered with steak,
And the stands were all covered with kidney.

# Ode to my Bike

O, let me list
the things I like
about my bike:
the seat
is neat,
each wheel
ideal.
The cogs and gears
deserve three cheers
and the pedals
medals!
The bell
works well,
the brakes
have what it takes.
The sturdy pump
you couldn't trump:
about the frame,
I feel the same.
Each nut and bolt
I so exult,
and oh, what stars,
the handlebars!
The whole design
is quite divine
there's truly
*nothing*
I don't like
about my bike.

# Freda, the Flat-footed Fairy

I'm Freda the flat-footed fairy,
My friends are the twinkle-toed lot—
They're slippery as butter,
They flit and they flutter
But look at these two feet *I've* got.

It's hard on a flat-footed fairy,
When others are nimble and quick,
To have two clodhoppers
Which really are whoppers,
Good only for giving a kick.

My friends are all frightfully flighty,
They frolic and fly fancy-free,
They're frothy and frilly
And frequently silly
And not at all clumsy like me.

My feet, like the lids of a dustbin,
Are big and as flat as can be
I can't be a leader,
I'm just poor old Freda,
The flat-footed fairy that's me!

## P.S.

But wait! Things are not always awful
And something that *does* make me laugh—
I can stamp on a walnut,
A big or a small nut,
And break it quite cleanly in half!

# Groovy Grandad

O Grandad, Grandad, please don't come
To pick me up from school
I think you look a fool
With that long ponytail you've got
Which *you* believe is cool.

Why can't you cut the daft thing off
Or hide it with a hat
Or give it to the cat?
But please don't come to my school with
A silly thing like that!

# Author Visit

We had a poet come yesterday,
He read his poems in an unusual way:
He said his words in a funny voice,
He'd whisper one line, then make a loud noise,
Shouting the next line and raising his arms
Like a magician reciting his charms.
He'd dance and prance and pull funny faces
And pause when we laughed in all the right places
We giggled, we screamed and we clapped at the end,
We cheered him and hugged him and called him our friend.
Now Poetry never will be quite the same
Since that fabulous frolicsome word wizard came—
I only wish I could remember his name.

# Xylophone

I love the sound of the xylophone—
like the banging of bones of an old skel-e-tone
Makes me think I'll leave my own
(one day) to musical science.